I0597289

Disappearing Stagecoach
by Michael Whalen

ISBN Paperback: 978-1-64873-548-6

Disappearing Stagecoach

by Michael Whalen

Acknowledgements:

Elias de Laveaga for helping edit and type

Liz McNett for helping edit and publish

1

"Griff, pull up your damn bandanna."

"What for? If we're gonna kill 'em all anyway, what's the use, boss?"

"Well, I'll tell ya. What if, by a miracle or somethin', one of 'em gets away? He could identify you, and you'd hang, you stupid son of a bitch. Now, pull up your bandanna; it's almost here."

The four horses were just trottin' along when they came around the bend, and there were four masked men with guns drawn, starin' right at 'em.

"Whoa, whoa, whoa!" yelled the driver as the stage came to a joltin' halt. "We ain't carryin' anything valuable, so you're just wastin' your time!"

"Don't lie to us, old man. We know you've got a shipment of gold, turquoise, and silver in that strongbox under your feet. So, first, throw down your sidearm, easy. Now the shotgun, and now haul that box out and toss it down. Griff, get them passengers out and frisk 'em."

Two old men climbed off the stage and emptied their pockets on the ground. One old man had a real nice derringer, and he threw it in the pile.

"Now get back on the stage!" barked Griff. "You two, put their stuff and that strongbox on that pack mule," ordered the boss.

He then rode up to the stage, shot the driver in the heart, stuck his pistol in the window, and likewise killed the other two passengers.

"Griff, tie your nag on the back and drive this rig out to where we picked out. Bury their bodies with the shovel off the packhorse, then turn the team loose. You other two, ride back and get them branches we cut and pull 'em up here to brush out all those tracks Griff is gonna make, and help him with the buryin'. Then, take a roundabout way back to Buckeye. I'll take the packhorse and go on back. Now get your asses goin'!"

2

Chip and Becky were sittin' and havin' coffee after breakfast when Becky said, "Hey, Chip, Kathy just flew in from Prescott. Let's see if she has a message on her leg."

Becky went out, put Kathy in the coop, and brought back a folded message that she proceeded to read to Chip: *Stagecoach missing in Buckeye with passengers and a strongbox. Go investigate.*

"Well, Becky, looks like I'll have to go and earn that ten dollars. Go on and fix me five days of vittles while I get saddled up."

While Becky got busy makin' up Chip's possibles pack, Chip was busy gettin' saddled up and harnessin' the packhorse with Old Clyde's help.

"Clyde, I gotta go to Buckeye and look into a missin' stagecoach. You know how to look after everythin' here, keep things runnin', and help Becky when she needs it. Don't know how long I'll be gone, so just carry on."

Clyde replied, "Chip, you be careful. You don't know what you're gettin' into, and yeah, I'll look after things here."

Chip walked the two horses up to the cabin, grabbed the .44 Yellowboy rifle, and strapped on a .44 sidearm. Puttin' everythin' on the packhorse, he turned and wrapped Becky in a big bear hug. He told her, "Becky, you and Clyde can handle things here, so I won't worry. Now, when I leave, send one of the homin' pigeons to Prescott sayin' I'm on my way."

They kissed in a big embrace, and Chip swung up into the saddle. "Come on, Elsworth!" he called, and rode toward the gate with his faithful canine companion trottin' alongside.

The ride to Buckeye was probably about four days, so Chip kept the horses at a steady pace all day, once stoppin' to rest and take a drink from a stream. When the sun started to go down, Chip pulled into a ravine that was hidden from the trail, fixin' a small fire for some coffee and beans and then hobblin' the horses in a place where they could rest up and graze. Next, Chip got his lariat off the saddle and made a great big loop on the ground, then put his ground cloth down and his saddle, got his wool blanket, and settled in.

The rope was to keep all sorts of critters away, and no snake would cross it. He settled in for a well-needed rest with

Elsworth to keep guard, and he was soon fast asleep. In the mornin', after some more coffee and hardtack, he saddled up and got back on the trail, aimin' to get to Wickenburg before dark. He hit Wickenburg right at dusk and headed to the livery stable, tellin' the hostler to water the horses and get 'em some grain and hay for the night. After finishin' up at the stable, he headed to the Bar-7 for a nice meal. The same old barkeep was there and recognized him.

"Marshal, what brings you out this way?"

"Well, I'm just passin' through to Buckeye to investigate a missin' stage," replied Chip evenly.

"Yeah, I heard somethin' about that. They say it was probably an inside job, but you know how they talk. Anyway, we got roast lamb stew and cornbread. That's okay?"

"You bet, old-timer! Then I'd like a bath and a room."

"You bet, Marshal, comin' right up."

The next mornin', Chip was up and on the trail by sunup and was makin' good time. That evenin', he pulled off the trail to get out of sight so any fire he had wouldn't be seen. Everythin' went well, and the next mornin', after a solid breakfast of coffee and hardtack, he was on his way again. He pulled into Buckeye early in the afternoon, sweatin' from the heat. He watered his horses and walked over to a run-down saloon, ordered a warm beer, and asked about work. One of the patrons, a Mexican, said he'd heard from the general store that the McCarthy brothers were lookin' for help.

"Well, amigo, where can I find their ranch?" inquired Chip.

"About seven or eight miles west," replied the Mexican. "It's the Slash P Bar brand."

Chip finished his beer, thankin' his new friend, and walked out, lookin' around. A dress shop, bank, gunsmith shop, livery stable, and general store—just about what he had expected. Swingin' back into the saddle, he took off west. He got to the ranch just before dark and found two men playin' with a bunch of puppies in the shade. Ridin' up, Chip greeted 'em with a friendly face.

"Howdy, heard in town you folks were lookin' for help."

"Maybe, maybe not," one of the men replied steadily. "So, just who are you?"

"I'm Chip Colfax, and I'm just lookin' for a place to do a little work."

"Well, Chip, I'm Matt, and this is my brother Mike. Our cook was just about to call us to supper, so you can eat with us if you like."

"Yup," said Chip. "Sounds good. I sure could use some home cookin'."

"Horse trough is down that way," instructed Mike. "You can water your horses and clean up. By that time, our cook will have supper ready."

Chip thanked 'em and headed for the water. Elsworth, meanwhile, exhausted from the day's endeavors, was lyin' on his belly warily, watchin' the pups play. All of a sudden, the pack noticed the newcomer, and within seconds, they were upon the older dog, playin' all around him. In surrender, the older dog sighed and laid his head down in defeat against the youthful army surgin' with energy around him.

They talked over the meal, and Chip decided they could be trusted. He told 'em he was a U.S. Marshal sent to look into the disappearin' stagecoach. Chip asked the boys if he could send a letter to Becky to tell her where he was. He didn't say that he was gonna have Becky get in touch with the U.S. Marshal's office in Phoenix.

After a good night's rest, he went to town the next day with instructions from the boys to pick up some beans, salt pork, and sugar at the general store. He let it be known that he had gotten a job at the McCarthy ranch, but still, no one but the twins and he knew he was a Marshal. The next day, he rode over west about a mile where the stagecoach road was, but to his disappointment, he found nothin' of interest.

3

Chip loaded the packhorse and started up the trail toward Kingman, got about halfway, and made camp way off the trail. He had a good night's sleep, got up at dawn, had coffee and some beans, and started back toward the ranch, lookin' at every nook and cranny on the trail. He was daydreamin' when he saw a branch off a mesquite tree. No mesquite trees were growin' anywhere nearby. He got off his horse and started searchin'. He found where someone had dusted the trail; that must've meant they'd used the mysterious branch to obliterate their tracks in an attempt to hide their trail. He led his horses and followed the almost-trail for seven or eight miles. He came to a rise, looked over it, and saw a big stagecoach. He was very careful. He checked everythin' out and found a grave big enough for three people. He took his horses over behind a small hill about a half a mile away and made camp. He stayed there two days, but nothin' showed up but some coyotes. He loaded up and went back to McCarthy's ranch. He told the boys what he had found and that he thought the outlaws would try the same thing again.

"Where is this stage, Chip?" Matt asked.

"About five or six miles south of Robin's Butte, and it's in one piece, just sittin' there all lonesome. I never touched the thing, and it's in a little canyon that you won't see unless you're lookin' right down on it," Chip replied.

"You got some kinda plan?" asked Mike.

Chip replied knowingly, "Well, if we leave it there and they strike again, we'll know where to look right off, won't we?"

"If it's an inside job, they'll have to know when a shipment is on board," said Matt.

"Right," said Chip, "and I think I can find out when that's gonna be."

The next day, Chip went to Buckeye and sent a letter to Becky, askin' her if she could see if the Marshal's office could find out when the next shipment was gonna be. Next came the waitin'. He waited and waited; two weeks went by, and nothin' happened. The next two weeks went by with no letter from Becky. Chip went to town every two days to check for mail. Still nothin'.

4

Wednesday mornin', Chip loaded up for Buckeye to check for a letter from Becky. It had arrived. He rode as hard as his horse could run back to McCarthy's ranch. Both boys were choppin' wood for cookin' and stackin' the rest for the winter heat.

He slid to a stop and said, "The robbery's today, boys, and the Marshal's office said to look for an engraved .45 derringer."

As they nodded their understandin', Chip added, "Oh, and by the way, boys, you're now U.S. deputy marshals."

"I always wanted to be one. What do we do, Chip?"

"Grab your horses and give me a fresh one. That stage is due anytime; we need to hurry, or we'll miss it."

Matt and Mike grabbed four fresh horses, saddled up, and put the panniers on a packhorse while Chip was gettin' his Yellowboy and the twins' .30-30s. They grabbed a few supplies out of the house and stuffed 'em in the panniers. They all mounted up and headed for the stage route. It took about an hour to get to the holdup spot. They all looked around and found where the bad guys had dusted the trail. Shakin' his head, Chip said, "We're too late. They already have the stage and any passengers that were on it."

Mike said to Chip, "Well, what do we do?"

Chip replied, "Well, we know where they're goin', so we'll head that way and then see what's to do."

Matt said, "Okay, let's get after 'em."

"We'll go as quietly as possible, and we'll stop every fifteen minutes or so and listen. We'll be able to hear 'em if we get close enough," instructed Chip.

They started without talkin' and rode for about fifteen minutes, then stopped and listened. No sound from anywhere. So, they went on, stoppin' and listenin', still nothin'. Chip said, "We're gettin' close, so when you get to that hill, you guys wait while I go up and look."

"You got it, Chip," said Mike.

"If they're there, I'll signal you two to come on up and spread out as you go, maybe thirty yards on each side of me, and get some cover before I challenge 'em, okay?"

Both Matt and Mike nodded, dismounted, tied all the animals to a mesquite bush, and settled to wait for a signal from Chip.

Chip took the Yellowboy from the scabbard and started easin' his way up the hill. When he got close to the top, he got down on his belly and crawled the last twenty feet or so. He peered over some rocks, and there they were, finishin' buryin' their passengers. He backed off and waved at the twins to come on up. Mike went left, Matt went right, and they eased their way up. Each of 'em settled behind some boulders about thirty yards away from Chip on either side.

Chip watched 'em get in position, then stood up and yelled, "Put up your hands! You're all under arrest!"

Griff and his accomplices grabbed their guns at their sides and fired toward Chip, but Chip had already ducked behind some rocks before they could get any range on him. In any case, he was over a hundred yards from 'em, well out of pistol range. The outlaws all made for some cover of their own. Griff ducked behind the stagecoach, the other two behind some rocks. Mike and Matt opened up with their .30-30 rifles, and it sounded like a war had broken out. The bad guys' pistols were no match against the brothers' rifles, so it was a lopsided kind of standoff until Matt hit a boot stickin' out from behind a rock that one of the bad guys was usin' for cover. The outlaw yelled and screamed as he fell sideways from his spot, and all three rifles cut him down with their deadly accurate fire. He fell dead, right where he had stood, but the other two men kept on firin' back at the deputies. The bad guys would both pop up, fire a couple of shots, then drop down behind their cover.

Chip said, "Wait till you think the guy behind the rocks is about to pop up again, and we'll all fire at the same time."

They sat and waited patiently. Then they saw the movement they'd been waitin' for come up from behind the rock, and all three cut loose at once, each one jackin' in a second round and firin' till they heard a yell. Just like his partner, he fell to the ground, dead from a shot right through his head.

"Okay, boys, hold your fire. Let's see if we can talk that last one into jumpin' ship." Then, turnin' to address Griff, Chip yelled out, "You behind the stage, come out with your hands up, or we'll shoot that stage into little pieces and you with it! You have sixty seconds startin' now!"

They waited for the time to run out. Just as they pointed their rifles, preparin' to send the outlaw to meet his maker, they saw his handgun hit the ground from behind the stage and a voice callin' out, "Don't shoot, don't shoot, don't shoot! I give up, and I'm comin' out. Don't shoot!"

Chip told the two boys to hold still and keep him covered while he circled their line of fire and came up behind the final bad guy. Once he had come up behind Griff, Chip said, "Get down on your knees and keep your hands in the air. There are two rifles pointed at your chest, and they have itchy trigger fingers."

Chip went up behind the bad guy, put him in shackles, and checked the other two, who were both dead. He then waved at the boys and yelled, "Bring the horses around and down here."

They both hollered back in acknowledgement and disappeared from view. Meanwhile, Chip looked around and saw that they had just finished buryin' the driver and the passengers who were on board.

Chip looked at Griff and said, "Well, man, looks like you're gonna hang. Where's the strongbox that's supposed to be on this stage?"

Griff said, "Don't know nothin' about no strongbox. We just wanted the guns and the valuables they had on 'em."

"Bullshit. This was a well-planned job, and you sure don't look like you're smart enough to pull it off on your own, but you will hang by yourself."

By this time, the twins were pullin' up on the scene. Matt asked if Chip had found the strongbox, as Mike looked all around.

"Someone else has made off with it," Chip informed 'em. "Yessir, there were more men in this gang, and we need to round 'em up like this one." He pointed at Griff. "He doesn't want to talk to us, so he's gonna hang by himself for all the killin'."

"I didn't kill anyone, and I'm not goin' down alone for this!" Griff snapped up to 'em from the ground.

Chip said, "Well now, let's start with what your name is and what you can tell us about this caper?"

"My name's Griff, but I don't know who the big boss is. We were just hired by someone by the name of Sawblade to help. I don't know what Sawblade's last name is, but I do know he hangs around Buckeye."

"You don't mean you don't know who the real boss is?" Chip said disbelievin'ly.

"No, sir, I swear I don't know who Sawblade gets his orders from, either, and that's the God's honest truth."

Matt said, "Get him up, and we'll take him over and shackle him to the stage. He won't be goin' anywhere then."

That finished, Chip said, "Boys, let's go over there out of earshot of him, and I'll tell you what I have in mind."

They went off a ways and huddled down as Chip started to instruct Mike. "I want you to ride to Buckeye. By the time you get there, it'll be way after dark. Go in real quiet, find the constable, and fill him in on everythin'. He'll probably be home. If not, wait for him and don't show yourself in town, okay?"

"Alright, Chip, but then what?"

"Have the constable find the stage manager and get two teams harnessed. Find two drivers, and the four of you head back here. You should get back by tomorrow mornin', and we'll go from there. Now saddle up and get a move on."

With that, Mike swung into the saddle and was off to Buckeye.

5

Matt grabbed the packhorse and started makin' some grub. "We need some nourishment 'cause we'll have to stand guard all night just in case any of the gang comes back lookin' for these three yahoos. I'll get some beans, salt pork, and some coffee goin' to help us through the night," said Matt.

After eatin' and feedin' Griff, Chip told Matt to get things cleaned up and then to take both their bedrolls up in those rocks at least fifty yards and spread 'em out.

"I'll take the first watch, and I'll wake you up when it's time for you to take over," Chip said.

Matt took the bedrolls and did what he was told, then rolled himself up in one and was asleep almost immediately. When he thought it was about two or three a.m., Chip went up to where Matt was and nudged him with his boot. Matt was instantly on his feet with his .30-30 in his hands.

"Easy there, Matt," Chip chuckled. "Everythin's quiet. It's just your turn to be on guard. I stirred up the fire and heated some coffee to get you started on the right foot. I'm gonna get some shut-eye."

With that, Matt was off and headin' for the fire for a nice cup of coffee.

Meanwhile, Mike had made it to Buckeye and found the constable, who rounded up the stage manager, and they were all headed out behind Robin's Butte with the two extra teams. Everythin' was goin' according to plan as they snuck quietly out of town.

The next mornin', Chip and Matt squatted by the fire after eatin' beans and pork belly when they heard the sound of the team comin'.

"Well, Matt, here they come," Chip grunted. "You get the packhorses loaded and saddle the other horses while I get Griff ready to travel."

When Mike and the rest got there, they immediately harnessed the teams to the stages, put Griff in the lead stage, and shackled him to the floor. They didn't want anyone to see him until they were ready for it, and they all headed back toward Buckeye with the bodies of the two bad guys in the second stage. About a mile out of Buckeye, Chip had 'em stop.

He pulled Griff out of the stage and put him on the stage manager's horse.

"You go in with the prisoner and the constable. I want you to circle town and come in quietly and get Griff in jail."

Then, go to the restaurant and eat. We'll wait here for one hour and then come in, makin' a big racket so everyone will soon know that we've got the stages back.

They loaded Griff on the stage manager's horse, and the four of 'em took off for Buckeye. Meanwhile, Chip reached into his pocket, pulled out his Marshal's badge, and pinned it on. That would sure as hell surprise a lot of folks who thought he was a cowhand out at McCarthy's. They waited an hour, then rode into town with the two vanished stagecoaches. They pulled the teams up to the stage office, helped unhitch 'em, and put the horses in the corral behind the office. Then Chip moseyed on down to the constable's office, where Mike, Matt, and the constable were. Chip gave a show of friendly greetin'.

"Howdy, boys, looks like everythin' went well."

It was the constable who replied. "Everythin's fine, and after you pulled in with the stages, we saw Sawblade hightail it into the bank, and he's still there."

"Well, we'd better go pay him a visit and ask him a few questions," Chip said easily.

The constable grunted in agreement. "Matt and Mike, cover us from here. It's only eighty yards, so your .30-30s will be fine."

Havin' almost reached the end of the road on this adventure, Chip didn't want the two boys to get hurt when they were close to the end of the trail.

"If it's all clear, I'll wave you boys over."

"You bet," they answered in unison.

6

Chip and the constable crossed the dusty street and approached the bank door. Chip leveled the Yellowboy, and the constable drew his sidearm and reached for the door. He looked over at Chip, nodded, and turned the knob, pullin' the door open.

Chip rushed through first, followed closely by the constable. Inside, behind the cage, was a young fellow of about twenty who asked, "Can I help you?"

Chip looked around and saw a closed door that said "Private." Chip whispered back, "Come out from behind that cage and get the hell out of here."

The boy looked at the two badges starin' at him and made swift steps through the swingin' door. He sprinted down the street, runnin' for his life.

Chip motioned toward the closed door, and both men moved forward. The constable reached for the knob, turned it, and jerked the door wide open. Chip stepped through the door with the Yellowboy held at the ready.

Lookin' surprised, Sawblade slowly raised his hands, as did the bank manager, who yelled, "Hey, man, is this a robbery or what?"

Ignorin' the bank manager's cry, Chip pointed his firearm at Sawblade. "If you're Sawblade, you're under arrest for murder and stage robbery. Put your hands behind you and don't move."

Sawblade slowly lowered his hands behind him but protested to Chip's accusation. "I have no idea what you're talkin' about. I ain't killed nobody!"

"Cover him while I put some cuffs on him," Chip said, now addressin' the constable.

Chip leaned the Yellowboy up against the chair and put the cuffs on Sawblade, then, headin' back to the bank door, he waved Matt and Mike over and hollered, "We got him!"

He went back into the bank office with Matt and Mike followin' and then addressed the bank manager. "Well, Mr. Suit-and-Tie, whoever the hell are you?"

"I'm Mr. Birdsong, and I own this bank and just about everythin' in town, so who the hell are you?" stated the bank manager indignantly.

"I'm U.S. Deputy Marshal Chip Colfax, and as you probably know, we've found the two stages and captured a fellow named Griff, who told us that Sawblade here is the ringleader, but also that he didn't know who the big boss was. You wouldn't know anythin' about that, would you, Mr. Birdsong?"

"No. Why would I know anythin' about stagecoach robberies and murder?" muttered Mr. Birdsong.

"Then you wouldn't mind us lookin' around, would you?" Chip asked, but without waitin' for a reply, he told the constable to keep an eye on 'em. Then, turnin' to the brothers, he said, "Mike, you look behind the cage out front, and Matt, that door ajar, you go see what's goin' on in there."

Both twins went to work. The constable still held his pistol on the bank manager and Sawblade, and Mike called out, "Nothin' out here, Chip!"

Matt pushed open the safe door all the way and saw two strongboxes sittin' in the back of the safe with the stage company's name on 'em. "Well, you'll have to explain these two sturdy boxes, Mr. Birdsong," Matt announced to the buildin'.

"I'm just keepin' 'em for the stage manager!" protested the bank manager.

"Yeah, I bet," growled Chip. "Now get out from behind that desk."

Chip moved behind the desk and started openin' drawers. The third one he opened, he froze. There lay a .45 derringer with engravin' on it. He reached in and retrieved it, lookin' at the engravin'.

"You, Mr. Birdsong, are under arrest for murder and stage robbery. Now put your hands behind you."

Chip cuffed him, picked up the derringer, reached into his pocket, and pulled out Becky's letter. "Read this!" he said to the constable and handed over the letter.

The constable read out loud. "Well, it says it's engraved with the name Horse P. Farnsworth."

Chip handed the little gun to the constable, who looked at it and said, "Well, I'll be damned. Okay, you two, let's go. You'll both be hung with Griff for this. Great work, Chip, you did a very good thing for this little town."

"Just doin' my job," sighed Chip, then turnin' back to the brothers. "Mike and Matt, get those strongboxes back over to the stage office so they can be on their way. I'll help lock these two up, and we'll go back to the ranch."

Back at the ranch, Chip started loadin' the packhorse for his trip back to his ranch. Elsworth, seein' they were about to leave, tore himself from the pack of puppies and took his place beside Chip.

"Boys, it was a pleasure workin' with you," Chip smiled as he shook the hands of the two brothers. "I'll see you get your ten dollars each. Right now, I'm headed home to see Becky."

He stepped into the saddle and waved a final farewell. "Thanks, boys, adios! Come on, Elsworth, let's go see Becky."

The End.

About The Author

Michael B. Whalen hails from Bloomington, Illinois, and pursued his education at Eureka College. Currently, he lives in Prescott, Arizona, where he cherishes the memories of his beloved wife, Dorthy, with whom he shared 50 wonderful years.

Michael finds joy in various hobbies, including golf, oil painting, karaoke, and playing Texas Hold 'em. He dedicated 38 years of his career as an electrical lineman for a power company in Arizona.

His debut book, Chip Colfax, Yellow Boy Rifle, is available on Amazon. Prescott, nestled in the picturesque Bradshaw Mountains, offers the charm of four beautiful seasons, making it an inspiring place for both life and literature.